THE
UGLY DUCKLING

Retold by LILIAN MOORE
from the story by Hans Christian Andersen

Illustrated by DANIEL SAN SOUCI

SCHOLASTIC INC.
New York   Toronto   London   Auckland   Sydney

To German with love
L. M.
To Manuel and Barbara Gomez
D.S.S.

ISBN 0-590-43794-1

Special contents copyright © 1987 by Scholastic Books, Inc.
Illustrations copyright © 1986 by Daniel San Souci.
All rights reserved. Published by Scholastic Inc.
Art direction by Diana Hrisinko. Text design by Emmeline Hsi.

12 11 10 9 8 7 6 5   0 1 2 3 4/9

Printed in the U.S.A.   08

First Scholastic printing, April 1987

It was summer and the country was beautiful. The wheat was yellow. The oats were green. And little hills of hay stood in the grassy fields. Here the stork marched about on his long red legs, talking Egyptian. (That's what his mother had taught him.) All around the fields there were forests, and in the forests there were deep lakes. Yes, it was beautiful in the country.

A great old house stood in the sunlight. And around the house was a moat—a deep and wide cut in the land that was filled with water.

From the walls of the house right down to the water, large leaves grew. Some of the leaves grew so tall a child could stand under them. It was like standing in a forest.

3

In the middle of this forest of leaves, a duck was sitting on her nest. Her eggs should be hatching soon. She had been sitting on them a long time and she was getting tired of it. Not many visitors had come to see her. It seemed as if the other ducks liked to swim around in the moat more than they liked to come and talk to her.

At last the eggs began to crack, one after another. The little ducklings stuck their heads out of their shells, crying, "Peep! Peep!"

"Quack! Quack! Quick! Quick!" the mother duck told them. And the baby ducks came out of the shells as fast as they could. They looked around at all the great green leaves, and their mother let them look as long as they liked, for green is good for the eyes.

"How big the world is!" cried the ducklings. They had so much more room now than in their shells.

"Don't think this is the whole world," said their mother. "The world goes way past the garden, and into the big field beyond. I have never been there, but that's what they say."

She stood up to look at her ducklings.

"Now, let's see. Are you all here? Dear me, no! The biggest egg is still there. How much longer is this to go on? I must say I'm sick of it!" And she sat down again on the nest.

"How are we getting on?" asked an old duck who came to pay her a visit.

"This egg is taking such a time," said the duck from her nest. "But do look at my other children. They are the prettiest ducklings I've ever seen!"

"Maybe you're sitting on a turkey egg," said the old duck. "That happened to me once. What a time I had! Those chicks wouldn't go into the water. I quacked and clacked at them, but it did no good. Let me have a look at that egg. Yes, that's a turkey egg all right! Just leave it there."

"I've been sitting this long," said the duck. "I may as well sit a little longer."

"Do as you please," said the old duck, and she waddled away.

At last the big egg cracked open.

"Peep! Peep!" cried the baby, and he tumbled out of the shell. The mother looked at him in surprise. He was so big and ugly!

None of the others looked like that, she
thought. Maybe he is a turkey chick after all. We'll
soon find out. He is going into the water if I have
to kick him in myself!

The next day was sunny and warm. Mother
Duck took her family down to the moat. Splash!
She was in the water.

"Quack! Quick!" she called to her ducklings.

Splish! Splash! One after another, they followed
her in. In a few moments all the chicks were in the
water, swimming nicely—even the big, ugly gray
one.

He's no turkey, thought the mother duck. See
how he uses his legs. And how well he sits on the
water. He's my own chick, I know. And he really
isn't so bad-looking when you get used to him.

She called again to the ducklings. "Quack! Quack! Quick! Quick! I'm going to take you out into the world now. We're going to the duck yard. Stay close to me so you don't get stepped on. And look out for the cat!"

Then they swam down the moat to the duck yard.

A fight was going on in the duck yard. What a racket! Two duck families were fighting over a fish head. And in the end the cat got it.

"That's the way it goes," said the mother duck. She would have liked some of that fish, herself.

"Come along now," she said to the ducklings. "Keep using your legs. Do you see that old duck over there? Bow to her. She's very important. She comes from a very grand Spanish family. That's why she's so nice and fat. See that red rag round her leg? She can be proud of that. It means her owner will keep her always.

"Come along now. Turn your toes out nicely.
Bow and say, 'Quack!'" And the ducklings did as
they were told.

All the other ducks in the duck yard looked at them. "Do we have to have them here, too?" they said loudly. "There isn't room for us. And look at the big one! Isn't he queer-looking? We don't want him around!" One duck flew over and bit him in the neck.

"Leave him alone!" cried the mother. "He's not doing you any harm."

"But he's so ugly!" said the duck.

"Your children are very pretty," said the grand old duck. "All but that big one! Does he have to look like that?"

"I'm afraid so," said Mother Duck. "But he's a good child and a good swimmer, too. I think he was in the egg too long. Anyway, he's a drake, and you don't worry so much about the looks of a son."

"Well, your other ducklings please me very much," said the old duck. "Make yourselves at home. And if you find a fish head, you may bring it to me."

So they began at once to feel at home.

All but the poor ugly duckling. He was bitten
and pushed and made fun of by the ducks and the
hens. As for the turkey cock, well, he had been
born with spurs, so he thought of himself as a great
prince. Now he puffed himself up and came at the
duckling with such a gobble! gobble! gobble! that
the poor thing did not know which way to run.

That was the first day. Every day after that was worse. The duckling was chased around the yard by everyone. His own brothers and sisters told him, "We hope the cat gets you, you ugly old thing!" Even his mother said she wished he were far away. The ducks bit him. The hens pecked him. And the kitchen girl who brought them their food kicked him out of the way.

It was too much. One day the duckling ran to the fence. Half running, half flying, he got himself over it. He frightened some little birds on the other side and they flew away.

It's because I'm so ugly, the duckling thought, and he closed his eyes. But he ran on, and he came at last to a swamp where the wild ducks lived. He stayed there all night, tired and frightened.

In the morning, the wild ducks flew up to have a look at the newcomer.

"Whatever kind of duck are you?" they asked. The little duckling bowed politely to all of them.

"How ugly you are!" they said. "Just don't try to marry into our family." Marry! The poor duckling wasn't thinking about that. He just hoped they would let him lie there in the swamp and drink a little water.

He lay there for two days and two nights.

Then along came two wild geese. They were young, not out of the egg very long.

"Hello!" they said to the duckling. "You're so ugly we sort of like you. Why not come with us and have a bit of fun? We know a swamp close by just full of wild geese. Very pretty little things. You're so queer-looking they might go for you!"

Bang! Bang! Two shots rang out. The two young
geese fell dead. Bang! Bang! went the guns again.
Whole flocks of geese flew up from the swamp.
Bang! Bang! Bang! Again and again the guns shot
them down. The hunters were everywhere, hidden
in the swamp and in the trees. The air was blue
with the smoke of their guns.

Then their hunting dogs came splashing
through the swamp. The frightened duckling tried
to hide his head under his wing. But suddenly a
big dog stood right beside him. The dog's red
tongue hung out and his eyes were wild. He
opened his great mouth and showed his sharp
white teeth. And then—splash—the dog went off
without touching the duckling.

How thankful the poor duckling was!

I'm so ugly, he thought, that even the dog can't stand me.

He lay there very still as the shooting went on and on. Late in the day it stopped. The duckling waited a long time before he dared to move. Then he ran from the swamp as fast as he could go.

He ran on and on, and that night he came to a broken-down little house. It was so old that it seemed about to fall over. But it did not know which way to fall, so it was still standing.

The door was hanging loose, and the duckling
saw a crack that he could slip through. And that is
what he did.

An old woman lived in the house with her cat and her hen. She called the cat Sonny. He could make his back go up. He could purr. And he could give off sparks if you rubbed his fur the wrong way. The hen had short legs and so she was called Dumpy. She was a good egg-layer, and the old woman loved her.

The next morning they found the duckling in the house. The hen began to cluck. The cat began to purr. And the old woman wanted to know what was going on. She did not see well, and she thought the duckling was a nice fat duck.

"Oh, good!" she said. "Now we will have duck eggs. If he's not a drake, that is. We'll have to wait and see."

So the old woman let the duckling stay on. He stayed in the house for three weeks, but he did not lay one single egg!

The cat and the hen were very bossy. They had not been out in the world, but they thought they knew everything. If the duckling opened his mouth to say anything, the hen clucked at him.

"Can you lay eggs?"

"No."

"Then be quiet!"

The cat asked, "Can you purr? Can you give out sparks?"

"No!"

"Then don't talk so much."

The duckling sat in the corner, feeling very gloomy. He thought about the world outside and the fresh air and the sunshine. Suddenly, he felt a great longing to swim in the water. He just had to tell the hen about it.

"What a crazy wish!" said the hen. "It's because you have nothing to do. Lay some eggs! Purr! Then you won't think about such silly things."

"But it's so wonderful to swim," said the duckling. "It's wonderful to put your head underwater and dive down."

"Wonderful?" cried the hen. "You *must* be crazy! The cat is clever. Ask him if he likes to swim. The old woman is wise. Ask her if she likes to put her head underwater!"

"You just don't understand," said the duckling.

"Indeed!" said the hen. "And if we don't understand you, who can, I'd like to know? Are you smarter than the cat or the old woman? I won't say a word about myself.

"Just be thankful for our kindness to you. You are lucky to be in this nice warm house with those who can teach you something.

"You are very foolish. And I tell you this for your own good. That's how you know your real friends. They tell you unpleasant things.

"Now why don't you try to lay some eggs or learn to purr and give out sparks."

"I think I want to go out into the world," said the duckling.

"Do as you please," said the hen.

So the duckling went on his way. It was so wonderful to swim. It was so wonderful to put his head underwater and dive down. But no matter where he went, everyone called him ugly and turned away from him.

Now the summer was over. The leaves in the woods turned yellow and brown. The wind took hold of them and danced them about. The sky looked gray, and the clouds were heavy with snow. A big black raven sat shivering on the fence, and calling, "Caw Caw." The cold got right into one's bones. The poor duckling had a bad time.

One evening, as the winter sun was setting, a flock of great white birds flew out of the bushes. They were swans, with long and graceful necks. The duckling had never seen any birds so beautiful.

With strange cries, the swans opened their great white wings and flew off to warm lands and open waters. And as they rose high, high in the air, a queer feeling came over the duckling. He turned round and round in the water to watch them fly. And he gave a cry so loud and strange that he frightened himself.

He could not forget those beautiful birds. Who were they? Where were they going? He did not know. He only knew that he loved them as he had never loved anyone before.

The winter grew colder and colder. The poor duckling had to swim around all day and all night to keep the water from freezing. But the hole in which he swam grew smaller and smaller. At last he was so tired that he gave up and lay still. And soon the duckling was frozen into the ice.

A farmer came by the next morning and saw
him. He broke the ice with his wooden shoe and
took the duckling home. There in the farmer's
warm house, the duckling came to life again.

The children wanted to play with him, but they frightened the duckling. He ran away from them— and landed in the milk pail. The milk splashed all over the room. The farmer's wife threw up her hands and screamed. More frightened than ever, the duckling flew first into the butter tub and then into the flour barrel. What a sight he was!

The farmer's wife screamed again and ran after the duckling with a poker. Laughing and shouting, the children ran after him, too. Thank goodness the door had been left open! The poor frightened duckling ran out of the house and into the bushes, and lay there in the newly fallen snow.

It would take too long and it would be too sad to tell how the duckling lived through the cold and bitter winter. He was back in the swamp, and there, one day, he felt the warm sun again. He heard the larks sing. It was spring.

He spread his wings. How strong they were now, and how easily they carried him along!

Before he knew it, he was in a big garden.

The apple trees were in bloom. The air was filled with the smell of lilacs, and the green branches of the lilac bushes hung down over a pond.

Suddenly, out of the bushes came three white swans, swimming lightly on the water. The duckling knew them at once. They were the beautiful birds he had seen in the sky.

A feeling of sadness came over him.

I must go to them, he thought. They will kill me because I am so ugly and I dare to go near them. But I don't care. Better to be killed by them than bitten by the ducks and pecked by the hens and kicked by the kitchen girl. So he flew into the water and swam to the beautiful birds. He saw them come to meet him with open wings.

"Kill me if you will!" cried the poor duckling,
and he bowed his head.

But what did he see in the clear water? The
water was like a mirror and he saw himself. He was
no longer an ugly duckling. He was a swan!

It doesn't matter if you are born in a duck yard if
you are hatched from the egg of a swan.

Now he was glad that his life had been so
unhappy when he was an ugly duckling. It helped
him understand better the joy of being a swan.

Some children came into the garden, and they threw bread into the water. One little child cried, "Look! There is a new one!" The others shouted, "Yes! There is a new one!" They clapped their hands and danced up and down and ran to get their mother and father.

They threw more bread to the swans. And they all said, "The new one is the most beautiful one of all!"

He was shy and hid his head under his wing. He did not know what to make of all this. He thought of how he had been laughed at by everyone. And now they said he was the most beautiful of all beautiful birds! He was so very happy, but not at all proud. A good heart does not become proud.

The bright sun warmed him. The lilacs bent down into the water as he went by. He lifted his long, graceful neck. His heart was filled with joy.

When I was an ugly duckling, he thought, I never dreamed I could be so happy.